Play Ball, Zachary!

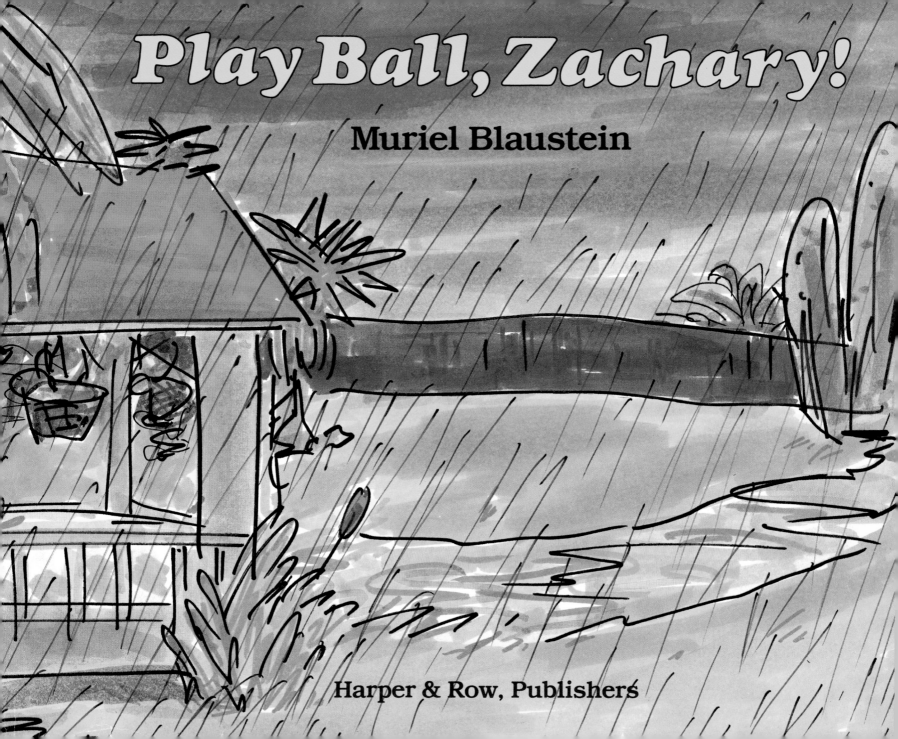

Play Ball, Zachary!

Muriel Blaustein

Harper & Row, Publishers

Play Ball, Zachary!
Copyright © 1988 by Muriel Blaustein
Printed in the U.S.A. All rights reserved.
1 2 3 4 5 6 7 8 9 10
First Edition

Library of Congress Cataloging-in-Publication Data
Blaustein, Muriel.
   Play ball, Zachary!

   Summary: Zachary the tiger cub is good at art and
reading and not good at sports, but he proves to his
athletic father that they can still do things together.
   [1. Fathers and sons—Fiction.   2. Ability—Fiction.
3. Tigers—Fiction]   I. Title.
PZ7.B61625P1 1988   [E]   87-45274
ISBN 0-06-020543-1
ISBN 0-06-020544-X (lib. bdg.)

The whole wet winter Zachary and his dad looked forward to doing new things. The first Sunday in spring Mr. Tiger said, "Let's go to the park, and…

Mrs. Tiger helped fill the truck.

Zachary liked to count,   read books,

ONE, TWO, THREE, FOUR

do jigsaw puzzles,

and paint pictures.

Zachary found out he did NOT like to play ball.

Zachary wanted to like the same things his dad did.

But Zachary still couldn't hit the ball.

Mr. Tiger said, "Maybe when you can move faster."

Zachary wanted to please his dad.

Mr. Tiger showed Zachary how to shoot baskets.

Zachary tried
harder, but...

he couldn't do it.

Mr. Tiger showed Zachary
how to punt.

Zachary ran as fast as he could, but the ball got away from him.

That night Mrs. Tiger said, "Well? How did your day with Zachary go?"

"Don't ask!" said Mr. Tiger. "I'm aching all over, and the worst part is…

And I was looking forward to having a good time with him."

Zachary was disappointed too.

The next morning when he went down to breakfast, only two places were set.

...and you know how bored and restless he gets when he has to stay in bed."

Zachary took Mr. Tiger's tray up to him.

He counted the steps so he wouldn't trip.

Mr. Tiger didn't look comfortable.

Zachary fluffed up his pillow and said,

"All right," said Mr. Tiger

When Zachary finished the story, Mr. Tiger said,

Next, Zachary painted a picture of Mr. Tiger at bat.

By lunchtime Mr. Tiger felt better.
He said, "Let's go downstairs."

Zachary helped him. They both thought,

After lunch Mr. Tiger wanted
to do a jigsaw puzzle.

Suddenly…

"Terrific, Dad!" said Zachary.
"I looked all over for that piece."

a ball bounced into their garden.

Zachary picked up the ball and tossed it with all his might.

The ball sailed over the fence.

"Maybe all you need is practice," said Mr. Tiger.

Now on sunny days, they do things they ALL like to do.

Except sometimes...

when Zachary does the things only HE likes to do.